ZACHARY

AND THE MAGIC SPECTACLES

A Book About a Boy Who Learns to be Nice

Rachel FreierMiller Sivek

AuthorHouse™
1663 Liberty Drive
Bloomington, IN 47403
www.authorhouse.com
Phone: 1-800-839-8640

Published by AuthorHouse 01/25/2012

ISBN: 978-1-4685-0762-1 (sc)

Library of Congress Control Number: 2011961395

This book is printed on acid-free paper.

authorHOUSE®

Once upon a time, there was a boy who made every kid afraid. All the kids tried as hard as they could to stay out of Zachary's way. If they didn't, he made them sorry.

Zachary teased Sarah about her pants.

He shoved Gary aside at
the fountain.

And he laughed at
Michelle when she stuttered.

But every October, Zachary was always too distracted to tease anyone. And the October of third grade was no exception. The school Halloween costume competition was soon approaching, and Zachary was designing his costume in the hopes that he might win another award.

A week before Halloween, Zachary stopped at his favorite costume shop on the way to school. Every year he bullied the old woman who owned the store even though he loved her costumes.

"Lady? Where are you?" Zachary yelled into the emptiness.

"I need help!" he roared.

A few moments later, the old woman walked slowly from the back. Zachary did not say hello or ask how she was feeling. He was annoyed by her slowness, so he rudely explained the concept for his Jimi Hendrix costume.

Before Zachary finished his explanation, she turned and walked away. She finally felt that it was time.

"Wait! Where are you going?" Zachary screamed after her. "I'm not done talking!"

The old lady soon returned, handed him a wooden box, and said, "These are what you need." Zachary wrenched the box open and saw a pair of purple polka-dotted spectacles.

"Excellent!" Zachary exclaimed excitedly. "I'm going to win!"
When he tried the specs on, they felt perfect. But when Zachary tried
to pull them off, they wouldn't budge. Panicked, he looked down and
found a note in the box.

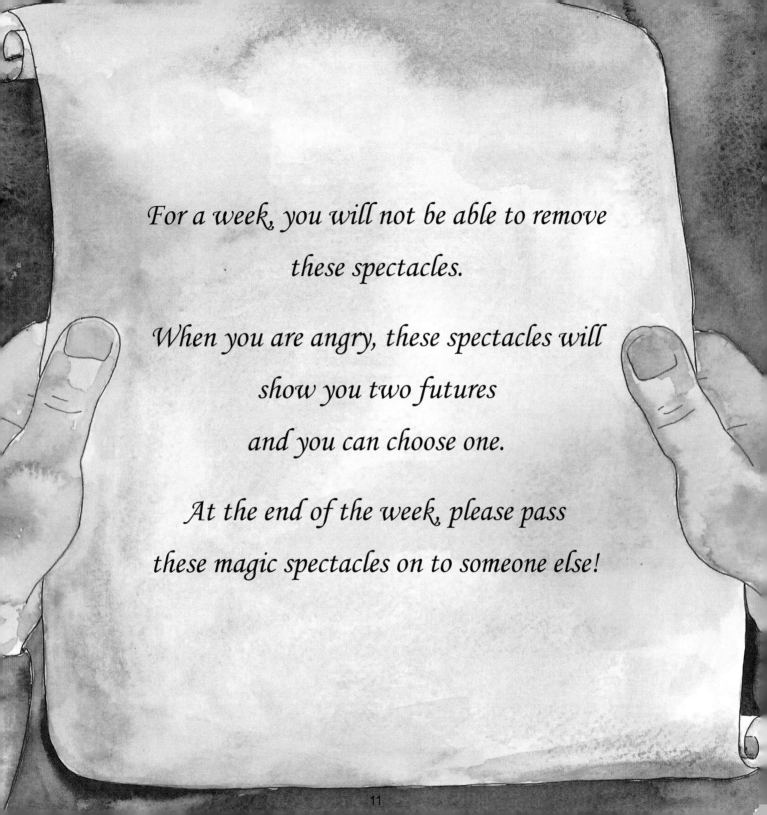

For a week, you will not be able to remove these spectacles.

When you are angry, these spectacles will show you two futures
and you can choose one.

At the end of the week, please pass
these magic spectacles on to someone else!

Zachary was puzzled and concerned. He threw his money down on the counter, stuffed the note back into the box, and ran out of the store.

At school, Zachary kicked his chair out from beneath the table, hurled his bag on the floor, and sat down next to Sarah. Zachary was angry that Sarah was staring at his new polka-dotted spectacles. Before he could yell at her, the specs began to quiver and the lenses went black. Time stopped.

Zachary: "What are you looking at?"
Sarah: "Nothing, it's just, those are… um… cool!"
Zachary: "You don't even know what cool is. You're weird no matter what!"

Zachary experienced everything Sarah felt. When Sarah's cheeks blushed, Zachary's blushed too. When Sarah's shoulders slumped with sadness, Zachary's slumped. Zachary felt something he did not recognize: embarrassment.

All of a sudden, Zachary's left lens dimmed and the right lens illuminated.

Zachary: "Why are you staring at my new spectacles?"
Sarah: "They're cool!"
Zachary: "Thanks. I like them, too! They're for my costume."
Sarah: "That's great! I hope you win again!"

For some reason, Zachary felt warm inside, and he could not help smiling. He was happy. Zachary enjoyed these feelings much more.

When the specs returned to normal and time continued on, Zachary still made fun of Sarah. He was mad at her, after all. But this time, he understood what it felt like to be in Sarah's place.

After class, Zachary went out for recess. He saw that Gary was happily swinging and decided that he wanted to swing, too. Though there was an empty swing next to Gary, Zachary wanted Gary's swing. The specs quivered, paused time, and showed Zachary two ways of getting Gary off the swing.

Zachary: "Move it, Fatso!"
Gary: "I'm not fat."
Zachary: "Yeah, you are. Get off before you break the swing!"

When Gary's face scrunched up with anger, Zachary's did too. Zachary felt Gary's resentment and pain, and his stomach hurt.

Next, the left lens dimmed and the right lens displayed a different future.

Zachary: "Gary, could I use the swing next?"
Gary: "Sure… I'll get off soon!"
Zachary: "Thanks!"

As the spectacles stopped quivering, and time resumed, Zachary realized that he could get Gary off the swing by being nice. Even so, he chose to be mean.

For the rest of the day, the spectacles made Zachary feel like a balloon filling with the pain of the people he teased. By the end of the school day, Zachary was so upset that he burst and made fun of the one person he never dared make fun of -- his teacher, Mr. Kougel. For the first time, Zachary deeply regretted his choice.

Mr. Kougel told Zachary to go to the principal's office and think about what he had done. Zachary thought about the feelings of embarrassment, resentment, and sadness. He remembered that he did not enjoy these feelings.

On his way home from the principal's office, Zachary saw Sarah fall off the sidewalk and land in the street. Zachary chuckled excitedly. He wanted to mock her and make her cry. He thought this might finally make him feel better. But before he could do anything, the spectacles interrupted him again.

Zachary: "Ha ha! What a klutz!"
Sarah: "Oh, uh, I just slipped."
Zachary: "You're so clumsy! Ha ha ha!"

When Sarah frowned, Zachary frowned too. When she turned her head away, Zachary did, too. For the first time, Zachary felt ashamed. He felt sick, and for some reason, his eyes and cheeks were wet.

The right lens lit up next.

Zachary: "Are you okay? Do you need help?"
Sarah: "Yes, I'm fine! Thanks."
Zachary: "You're welcome. I'll see you tomorrow at school!"

When Sarah smiled, Zachary smiled. He felt her gratitude, and he enjoyed her happiness.

Once again the specs grew still. This time Zachary made a new choice. He decided that he was tired of feeling pain and wanted Sarah to feel happiness. Zachary chose to help Sarah. She was shocked, but pleased. Zachary felt happy when he saw her smile, and he realized that being nice made him feel good, too.

During the next week, the magic spectacles showed him how his actions affected others. Seeing the future helped him make people happy rather than sad. Slowly, Zachary became friends with the people who once feared him. They began to trust him.

Rather than tease Gary for being alone at recess, Zachary played with him.

Rather than make a joke about Sarah's haircut, he complimented her.

And rather than laugh at Michelle for her math error, he helped her.

Finally, it was Halloween, and Zachary's groovy costume won him another trophy. After the trophy ceremony, Zachary's new friends Gary and Sarah invited him to trick-or-treat.

Zachary had never trick-or-treated with friends. He loved the company.

Back at home, Zachary, Gary, and Sarah emptied their full pumpkin baskets onto the floor. They sorted and traded their candy. As Zachary looked down at the piles of delicious candy, the magic spectacles fell off his nose. Surrounded by his new friends, Zachary saw what the spectacles had given him.

At school the next day, there was a new student in Zachary's class named Margaret.

She sang a song during the quiz.

She put a tack on someone's chair.

And she told Zachary that he smelled like peas.

Zachary felt shame, he felt embarrassment, and he felt resentment. He finally understood how bad it felt to be teased, and he knew that Margaret desperately needed the specs. When Margaret was not looking, Zachary slipped the box into her backpack. You know what happens next!

Discussion Questions
1) Have you ever been bullied? If so, how did you feel?
2) What did Zachary learn from the spectacles?
3) Have you acted like Zachary before?
4) If you saw someone who was being bullied, what could you do to help?
5) If you had a pair of polka-dotted spectacles, what would you see and do?